Book Club Edition

WALT DISNEY's
Robin Hood
and the Golden Arrow

Robin Hood and Little John were hiding out
in Sherwood Forest.

The two outlaws had tricked Prince John.
They had taken his gold and given it back
to the poor people he had robbed.

While Robin Hood stirred the kettle of soup,
Little John was hanging up the washing.

Suddenly their good friend Friar Tuck
came rushing down the road from Nottingham.

He tasted the soup.

Then he said, "Have you heard the news?
Prince John is holding an archery contest.
All the archers in the kingdom are invited.
And Maid Marian will give the golden arrow
to the one who wins the contest."

Robin Hood was very happy to hear the news.

"I will go to that contest," he shouted.
"And I will win the golden arrow and see Maid
Marian too!"

"Wait a minute, Robin," said Friar Tuck. "How
can you go to Prince John's contest? All of his
soldiers will be waiting for you!"

"Don't worry," Robin answered.
"No one will know who we are.
We will wear disguises."

Robin dressed up like a long-legged stork.

Little John dressed himself to look like
a nobleman of high rank.

Who would believe they were
really two famous outlaws?

On their way to the archery contest, they met the Sheriff of Nottingham.

"Why, good morning, Sheriff," said Robin. "What an honor to meet you here."

"And a good morning to you, my fine friend," answered the sheriff.

He never guessed that he was speaking to Robin Hood!

As Robin and Little John drew near the castle grounds, they met all sorts of people.

Everyone in the kingdom was coming to Prince John's archery contest.

In the center of the field stood a very tall throne.

Prince John was sitting there beside Sir Hiss, his advisor.

Prince John smiled.

"At last we are going to capture that outlaw Robin Hood," he said.

"Are you quite sure, sire?" asked Sir Hiss.

"Of course I am sure. Robin Hood loves Maid Marian. So I know he will come and try to win the golden arrow."

"You should be careful," warned Sir Hiss.

"Remember how Robin Hood and Little John stole the rings right off your fingers . . . and the wheels right off your coach."

"Silence, Hiss!" roared the prince. "And don't ever let your head be higher than mine!"

The line of archers marched across the field.
They had come from all over the kingdom.
Each archer carried a stout-looking bow.

At the end of the line walked a tall archer on stilt-like legs.

He was right in front of the sheriff.

Little John did not stay with Robin Hood.

He went straight to Prince John and bowed low before him.

"And who might you be, sire?" asked Sir Hiss.

"I am Sir Reginald, Duke of Chutney," answered Little John. "I have come to pay my respects to Prince John."

"Please sit down, sir," said the prince. "We do not often get such fine visitors."

Little John sat down
—right on Sir Hiss.
"Sir Chutney! You
have taken MY seat,"
said Hiss.

"Hiss! Get out
of here!" commanded
Prince John. "You are
no longer needed.

Go out onto the field and keep
your eyes open for that villain
Robin Hood."

Just then Maid Marian came
up to the throne with Lady Kluck.
They bowed to Prince John.
Then they sat down next
to the royal throne and waited
for the archers to file past.

One archer, taller than the others, handed
a flower to Maid Marian.

"It is a great honor," he said, "to be
shooting for a lovely lady like you."

Then he winked at her and walked away.

"My goodness, Kluck," said Maid Marian.
"The eyes of that archer
do look familiar."

Suddenly the trumpeters on the castle tower
blew their horns.

The archery contest was about to begin.

The contest master walked toward the throne.
He stopped in front of Prince John and held
up the golden arrow on its purple cushion.

The archers lined up in a long, straight row,
ready to shoot.

At the signal each one, in turn, let his arrow
fly toward the target.

The sheriff and the stork were the best.

The sheriff's arrow went right into the center of the yellow circle.

But Robin Hood's arrow went right into the circle too.

The first match had ended in a tie.

Little John looked at the prince.

"Did you see that?" he asked. "That long-legged archer is very good!"

"Indeed he is." The prince smiled. "I just wonder who he can be. Not many men can shoot as well as the sheriff."

On the field the sheriff and Robin Hood
were getting ready for their next shot.

"I hear you are having trouble catching
that rascal Robin Hood," said the long-legged
archer.

"Oh, it's no trouble," said the sheriff.
"He's scared of me, that's all. But if he
dares to come here today, I will spot him—
even in one of those silly disguises."

"Attention, everyone!"
shouted the contest master.
"The sheriff and the stork
from Devonshire will shoot
again. But first they must
move back thirty paces."

The sheriff bowed
very low.

Then the stork bowed,
at the same time waving
to Maid Marian.

Maid Marian waved back.
She was smiling happily.
Now she was sure that she
knew who the long-legged
archer was.

"I think you like that tall archer,"
said Prince John.
"Oh, yes!" answered Maid Marian, and
her face turned red. "That is, he makes
me smile."
But the prince was not smiling. For
now he was sure that he knew who the
long-legged archer was.

It was the sheriff's turn to shoot again.

This time his arrow went too high.

But the target holder quickly raised
the target.

The arrow landed in the bull's-eye!

Next, the stork took his turn.

The long-legged archer aimed carefully and
stretched his bowstring tight.

His arrow flew straight to the bull's-eye.

It knocked the sheriff's
arrow to the ground.

The stork had won!

Friar Tuck roared with delight.

"He did it! He did it!"

All the villagers cheered with him.

The long-legged stork from Devonshire
was the hero of the day.

Maid Marian hugged
Lady Kluck.

Prince John
whispered an order
to the contest master.

The contest master
whispered the order
to the captain
of the rhino
guards.

Robin Hood walked to the throne and
bowed to Prince John.

"Archer," said the prince, "you have won
the contest. Now you will get your reward!"

With a quick slash of his sword,
the prince tore off Robin's stork
disguise.

All the rhino guards grabbed Robin and
tied him round and round with ropes.

"Robin Hood, I have been waiting to catch
you," shouted Prince John. "Now that I have
you, you shall die!"

"Oh, no, Prince John,"
cried Maid Marian. "Spare
his life, I beg of you."

"Why should I?" asked the prince.

"Because I love him," Maid Marian
answered softly.

While Maid Marian
was talking, Little John
quietly sneaked behind
the throne.

All at once Prince John felt something
sharp sticking into his back. And a strong
hand pulled his collar tight around his
neck.

"All right, Prince," whispered Little John.
"Tell your men to let Robin Hood go."

"Untie the prisoner!"
shouted the prince. "Let
him go at once, I say!"

Suddenly Robin Hood was free again.

The sheriff could not believe what
was happening.

Before Prince John could change his mind,
Robin rushed to the platform and grabbed Maid
Marian and Lady Kluck.

Running behind the throne, Robin Hood took
the dagger from Little John.

Then he cut the rope that held the cloth
roof over the throne.

Down it crashed, trapping the prince,
the sheriff, and all of the guards.

While the prince and his men struggled
to get free, Robin and his three
friends ran off
as fast as they
could go.

They did not stop running until they were
across the river, safe in the shelter of the
forest.

"You see," said Robin. "I did win the contest."

And that was how Maid Marian and Lady Kluck
came to join Robin Hood and his band of outlaws
in Sherwood Forest.